D1515226

For my baby brother, Orian, my first delighted reader, whom I will forever love and remember.

Bala Kids
An imprint of Shambhala Publications, Inc.
2129 13th Street
Boulder, Colorado 80302
www.shambhala.com

Text © 2022 Allysun Atwater
Illustrations © 2022 Stevie Lewis

Cover art by Stevie Lewis
Design by Kara Plikaitis

All rights reserved. No part of this book may be reproduced in any form
or by any means, electronic or mechanical, including photocopying, recording,
or by any information storage and retrieval system, without permission
in writing from the publisher.

9 8 7 6 5 4 3 2 1

First Edition
Printed in China

☺This edition is printed on acid-free paper that meets the American National Standards
Institute Z39.48 Standard.
♻Shambhala makes every effort to print on postconsumer recycled paper.
For more information please visit www.shambhala.com.
Bala Kids is distributed worldwide by Penguin Random House, Inc.,
and its subsidiaries.

Library of Congress Cataloging-in-Publication Data
Names: Atwater, Allysun, author.
Title: I am thinking my life / Allysun Atwater.
Description: Boulder: Shambhala, 2021. | Audience: Ages 4–8 | Audience: Grades K–1
Identifiers: LCCN 2020023772 | ISBN 9781611808971 (hardback)
Subjects: LCSH: Self-perception—Juvenile literature. | Self-consciousness (Awareness)—
Juvenile literature.
Classification: LCC BF697.5.S43 A89 2021 | DDC 155.4/191—dc23
LC record available at https://lccn.loc.gov/2020023772

I AM THINKING MY LIFE

Allysun
Atwater

illustrated by
Stevie Lewis

Shorewood-Troy Public Library
650 Deerwood Drive
Shorewood, IL 60404
815-725-1715
www.shorewoodtroylibrary.org

I am thinking my life.

Every day.

I am creating a universe.

I am communicating with the world.

I think stars. I see stars.

I am stars.

I think myself smiling. I see myself smiling.

I am smiling.

I am sculpting my world. I am clay. I am motion. I am light.

I am what I think.

I am planning my world.

I breathe meaning into my life through my thoughts and then my actions.

I am the architect
of my dreams.

I think myself joyful.
I see myself joyful. I am joyful.

But then sometimes, I think storms. I see storms.

I am storms . . . and thunderclouds . . . and tears.

But then, even though it's difficult,
I search and I search inside myself and . . .

There it is!

I think sunshine! I see sunshine!
I am sunshine!

And the clouds and the thunderstorms roll away from my mind. They have no power! And I can think anything!

I think myself dancing.

I see myself dancing.

I am dancing.

I think myself building.

I see myself building. I am building.

I think myself drawing.
I see myself drawing.
I am drawing!

And look at my creations!

I think beauty. I see beauty. I am beauty.

I think affection. I give affection. I am affection.

I am powerful. I am radiant.

I am loving.

I am creative.

I am seeing.
I am becoming.

I am thinking my life!
I am thinking my world!

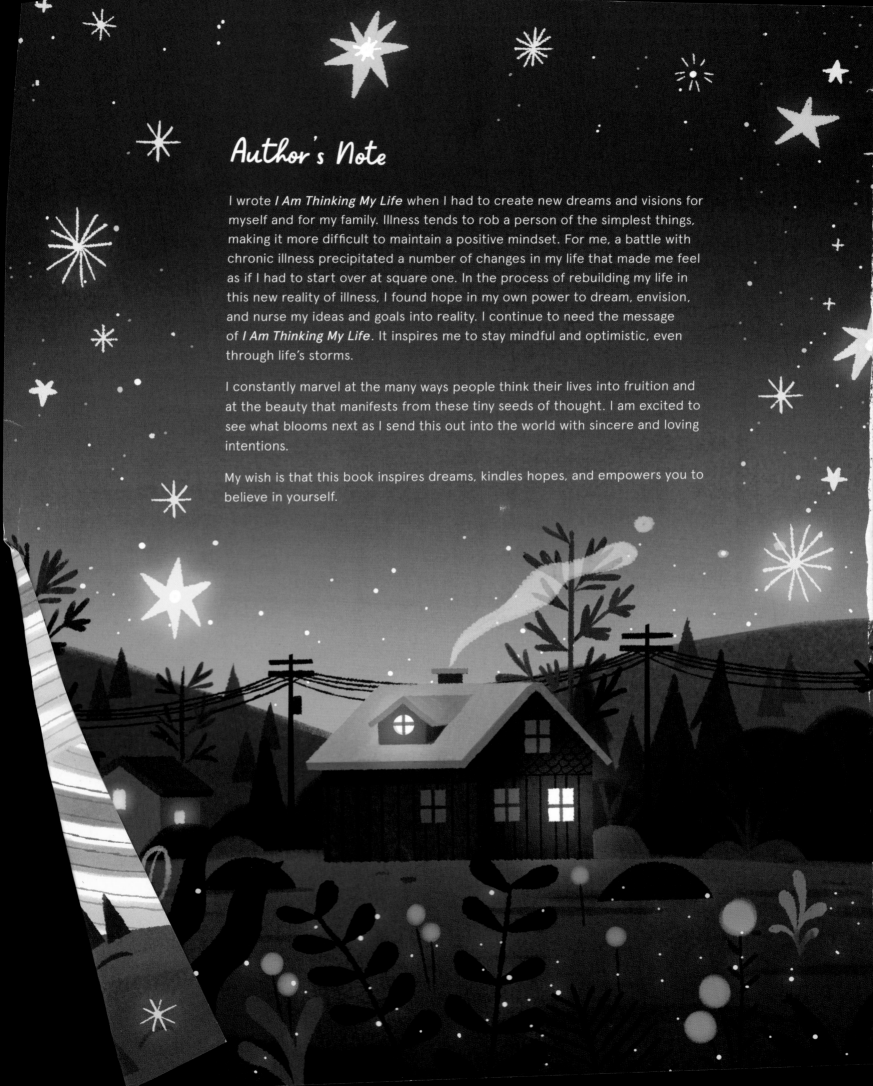

Author's Note

I wrote *I Am Thinking My Life* when I had to create new dreams and visions for myself and for my family. Illness tends to rob a person of the simplest things, making it more difficult to maintain a positive mindset. For me, a battle with chronic illness precipitated a number of changes in my life that made me feel as if I had to start over at square one. In the process of rebuilding my life in this new reality of illness, I found hope in my own power to dream, envision, and nurse my ideas and goals into reality. I continue to need the message of *I Am Thinking My Life*. It inspires me to stay mindful and optimistic, even through life's storms.

I constantly marvel at the many ways people think their lives into fruition and at the beauty that manifests from these tiny seeds of thought. I am excited to see what blooms next as I send this out into the world with sincere and loving intentions.

My wish is that this book inspires dreams, kindles hopes, and empowers you to believe in yourself.

Author's Note

I wrote *I Am Thinking My Life* when I had to create new dreams and visions for myself and for my family. Illness tends to rob a person of the simplest things, making it more difficult to maintain a positive mindset. For me, a battle with chronic illness precipitated a number of changes in my life that made me feel as if I had to start over at square one. In the process of rebuilding my life in this new reality of illness, I found hope in my own power to dream, envision, and nurse my ideas and goals into reality. I continue to need the message of *I Am Thinking My Life*. It inspires me to stay mindful and optimistic, even through life's storms.

I constantly marvel at the many ways people think their lives into fruition and at the beauty that manifests from these tiny seeds of thought. I am excited to see what blooms next as I send this out into the world with sincere and loving intentions.

My wish is that this book inspires dreams, kindles hopes, and empowers you to believe in yourself.